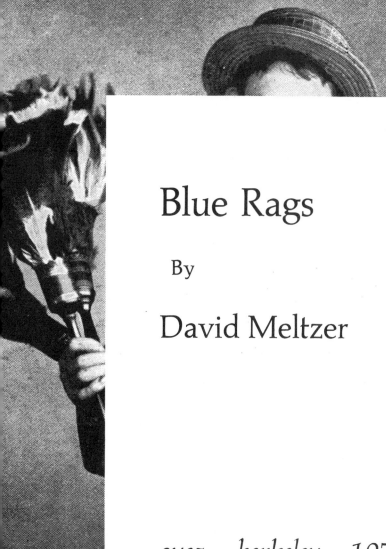

Blue Rags

By

David Meltzer

oyez   berkeley   1974

For Radio,

A Romance.

Pre Face

Throat
choked.
Adam's
                    apple.
Closed.
Taught to sing flowers.
But no more. Sorry.
                    Flowers
Outside.
Throat's inside
Voice is let out.
No more wings.
Singing is hard.
Let's talk.
Throat
                    choked.
No longer for you or her.
Await nothing.
Four sides of fear.
Crowned.
                    Throat
tunnel a book looks down.
Into the meander.
No longer you or her.
Nothing.
Eight sides of self.
Slashed.
Ribbons on the dome's gold pole.
Wind bags turn into flags.
Tatter. Color fades. Outside too long.
                    Eyes
Match eyes.
I expect another day.
Anyway.
Let's talk.

Talk of elegance. Grace. Style.
Above all others. Who drown.
Arise.
In cement. Stuck in earth.
Arise.
Clods. Hopeless. Arise.
A rumor. A mysterious stranger.
Alights. An appearance.

Talk of elegance. The old days.
Rising above all others.

Always clean.
Operating room floor.
Cell.
Black & red tiles.
This closet. A window.
Big enough to hold screams
You say are poems.

Who writes these verticals.
Held back.
Who is it in there.
Wiring these poems.
Peek through.
Who.
Held back.
Verticals.
Black cloth over eyes.
Gaggle of kitchen gossip.
Downstairs.
Scrape against peg-board
Fingernails wear down.

The lot. Held all time.
Together in its fences.
No one to see it. Go.
But it was. There.
The lot.
Forever.

Inside news. Locale. The page.
How many times. Does the sun go. Apart in our face.
To die. Without once. Ever.
What a shame.

Did it hurt.

How can I. On TV. So easy. Yawn.
Dull. Death all over the place.
Dismiss. Dismantle. Blood holes.
How many more deaths.
How many more bullets.
How many more. To restore. The page.

Tell it to the kids.
Bang bang.
A song.

Three Amulets

Slow. To go against it.
The word. The page.
Marks. On the white.
My whole life.
Marked by words.
Slow to go against it.
To go against their hard shapes.
To wound the page with metal.
Holes in the paper.
I wave in your face.
We follow each other.
I'm behind you. At night.
You're behind me when I stand up to leave.
We face each other on the page.

Invoke. Invoke.
Invoke. Invoke.
It begins to look Swedish.
Or German.
Her blond hair.
Her black hair.
Roots of her blood.
Perfume of cups.
Inner white thigh.
Soft silk hidden from the sun.
Teeth. Tongue.
Prospects of song.
Invoke. Invoke. Invoke.
Her bite.
Against night.
Pulls sheets apart.
Spine tangle. Knots & eyes.
Paper Japanese mask.
Her tongue pushes through.
A hole in the center of air.
Poems in her hair.
Nest.
Blood of her mystery.
Bloom of her history.
In her stars we rest.
In the dark.
Her body opens.

3.

You do.
That hoodoo.
You do it. In the dark.
Or in the bright hot.
Palms & corked polly.
Scorched parrots.
Rum bubbling on the dirt floor.
Each cloud overhead a loa.
Shadow of your prayer.
Wicker knots.
Drums unhinge.
Each loa wandering until you voice it.
You do that hoodoo.
We do it. Apart. In the dark.
Or in the bright hot.
On or off the page.
A yellow horse tiptoes the veve's curls.
Your sunglasses frame a falcon.
Rum bumblers drown in jewelry.
Oceans dumbfound the dancers.
But humble souls in white abide.
Hold the sun above their pure minds.
Humble souls in white clouds.
Darken as you leave the shrine.
Black-winged rooster ducks behind an oil drum.
We turn each other inside out.
You do that. We do that. Hoodoo.

Upon the open wave.
Whereupon the ocean is a recording.
Her radio tuned to news.
Her mouth pressed upon his.
Opens.
We explore breath.
Our germanies.
Upon the open wave.

Oh so low.
So lost. So cold.
Who'll buy my flowers.
Snow on a shrine's dome.
Strike a match.

Knee on wood plank.
Far Rockaway shul.
Daven, David.
Break the ice.
Who is inside will be freed.
Heart knot opening.
Everybody doubled. Othered.
Somebody else.
Not the same.
Restore my sight.
So low. So lost.

Old tapdancer.
Salt statue.
Lights action camera.

Upon the open.
She doth arise.
Eyes hold dream.
Mouth metal.

She doth arise to light through Rembrandt's window.
Fiction is across the river.

Ariseth into light
Her lover turns against.

Close the book.
Arise to dream's horizon.

Radio

Y : Blue grey over you.
      Impossible to tell you anything.
      You know it all, you know.

H : I know nothing or why would I sit
      Asking you to tell me something I want to know.

Y : I'm the person who is always asleep.
      Not one to asks question of.
      Because I talk in my sleep I am not an oracle.
      I know nothing.

H : No.
      I've read all your books.
      I've heard you speak before crowds.
      Everyone agrees you are the wisest of all.
      A phenomenom.

Y : I slept through it all. That's what I'm telling you.
      I slept throught it all. That's the truth.
      I know nothing.

It is all radio & television.
Peace talks. Watergate. Fuel Crisis.
Julius & Ethel Rosenberg.
A mountain of rose petals.
What's left of Brooklyn.
Yellow Pages.
Nothing to hold on to.
History.
Easy as pie.

It stays.
We couldnt.
Dust is the song.
We couldnt.
I couldnt.
Dust on all the coleus.
Floor to floor walls.
Electricity.
Record on the turntable.
Sonny Rollins. 1958.
It isnt all over.
There can never be.
Another now.
It stays.
Here.
Cracked.
Dust is what a time machine coughs back.

I spy, we spy.
I must know why.
Information.
She ariseth from bed.
Propelled.
Door opening. Sonata.
Hello, are you there.
Yes, I am here.
Dial tone. Swallows her ear.
Who do you wait for.
At the other end.
Who is there.

The clear.
Ever more.
Even now.
Start & end here.
Along an edge.
Leaf or lip of brass jar
Placed on a dark shelf.
Formal.
No picture. No music.

Aftermath.
Along the edge of a word.
Cuts through.
Knife blade tears spider web.
All soaring trapped.
Language lack.
No one can say it.
If only you could.
Know it with me.

Radio

Couldnt.
Didnt you try.
Why. Impossible. She.
What about right & wrong.
She. Nobody else. I couldnt.
Oh well. Passé. All over. You know.
I dream we are movies.
Ah it's late.
Or books of pop-up aquarium underwater ballet.
    Graceful.
No, no. Re-run. Re-run. Re-run.
Back through time.
Corn.
Emblem. Despair. Truth.
Lofty. Corn. Re-run. Re-run.
Re-run. Re-run. Re-run.

I had no. All the time. That way. Blank.
They open doors for my breath.
A shadow too fast.
Match-flare. Eye opens. Shuts.
I had no. Every second. No comfort.
She turns. She turns.
I had no.
All my words. Your words. Books. Strobes.
Wont you listen. I had no.
Our song. Silence. She opens the gate.
No house beyond it. A movie-lot.
Wheatfield. Overgrown weed field.
Helicopter. 6 oclock news. I had no.
Her teeth at my feet.
Blood at the edges.
All the time. That way. Blank.

Sense data. Broken. Down. Old.
Smile. Cracked lip.
La bas. Lowest. Lower.
Tokay's okay. Pass the bottle.
Pull fuel out of green glass.
Tender scour. Flesh is dust.
What's the use.
Sense data. Blocked.

Radio

I must do it.

Did you read the drumroll. About the zim & zoom. Or for that matter jazz. How it moves inside even when I stand still. A theory linked with the Greeks. Outside too with faces & mouths. Are they singing.

Do it again on the page.

Listen to my music. It is 4 square. A building on fire. They dive out of windows. We read their names on the ground.

It's been done.

Smoke. Light. Inhale. Exhale.

Gets you. Out there. Where it's all happening.

Sure you remember her. The one I told you about back then when I opened the other end & Africa was there.

We weren't even kids together.

She comes from the other side. They all do.

We bought different goods.

No mystery. Just doorways. In & out.

Her face against the window. Waiting. In smoke. Gone.

I always ate Cheerios. Everything is turned into food. On TV you see it all.

Or the other one who patted my butt in a club painted black on Sunset Boulevard.

Remember those Captain Marvel annuals with cardboard covers. I collect anything made out of paper I can read words off.

Never. She had a big nose. Wooden skin. Erotic. Purple Sweater. Waves. Hello. Goodbye. Nothing in between. I never touched her. She shut the door. Too late.

Blue rags are what you get when you get there.
It's no longer a he or a she.
A skeleton that won't dance.
No looking ahead. Or back. Or down.
Lights out. White orbs. Blank.
Can't see through. Nothing inside.
A ration of blue rags. Tin cup.
Nobody around for miles.
When you get there. There's no doubt.

(1974)

Blue Rags has been printed in two editions:
The trade editions consists of 1,000 copies
in wrappers and 250 copies bound in cloth;
an edition of 100 copies has been
printed letterpress and bound by hand
by Graham Mackintosh and are numbered
and signed by the author.